# I Love You!
## A Bushel & A Peck

*taken from the song "A Bushel and a Peck"*

*words and music by*

## Frank Loesser

*pictures by*

## Rosemary Wells

HarperCollins*Publishers*

Thanks to Rochelle Schiffbauer and Larry Rakow at Kidstamps, and with special

thanks to Johanna Hurley

—R.W.

Library of Congress Cataloging-in-Publication Data is available.

ISBN 978-0-06-028549-4 (trade bdg.) — ISBN 978-0-06-028550-0 (lib. bdg.) — ISBN 978-0-06-443602-1 (pbk.)

Typography by Martha Rago

❖

14 15 16 17 18  SCP  10  9  8

First Edition

For Alexia Cable Hain
—R.W.

I love you,

a bushel and a peck,

A bushel and a peck

and a hug around the neck,

Hug around the neck
and a barrel and a heap,

Barrel and a heap
and I'm talkin' in my sleep

about you.                   About you?

About you!

My heart is leapin'!

I'm having trouble sleepin'!

'Cause I love you,

a bushel and a peck,

y'bet your pretty neck I do.

Doodle oodle oodle,

doodle oodle oodle,

a-doodle oodle oodle ooo.

I love you

a bushel and a peck,

a bushel and a peck

and it beats me all to heck,

Beats me all to heck
how I'll ever tend the farm,
ever tend the farm
when I wanna keep my arm

about you.

About you?

About you!

The cows and chickens
are going to the dickens!

'Cause I love you,
a bushel and a peck,
y'bet your pretty neck I do.

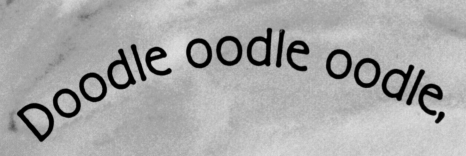

Doodle oodle oodle,

doodle oodle oodle,

# A Bushel and a Peck

*Words and music by* **Frank Loesser**

*Light Bounce Tempo*

| G | D7 | G | D7 | G | A7 |

I love you a bu – shel and a peck a bu – shel and a peck and a
I love you a bu – shel and a peck a bu – shel and a peck tho' you
I love you a bu – shel and a peck a bu – shel and a peck and it

| D | D7 | G | Em7 |

hug a - round the neck Hug a - round the neck and a bar - rel and a heap
make my heart a wreck Make my heart a wreck and you make my life a mess
beats me all to heck Beats me all to heck how I'll ev - er tend the farm